Little Red Riding Hood

Welcome to Fairytale Village,
where stories happen every day.
Today we're reading Little Red Riding Hood's
adventure, but if you look closely you might
spot some other stories happening in the background.

Keep your eyes open for a brother and sister,
lost in the woods, and for a wicked witch,
waiting in her gingerbread house…

*For Frances Mary — happy first birthday. Don't be scared of
the wolf, he doesn't live in Spondon. Love from Alison — A. J.*

For Emily & Vicky, thank you — J. L. H.

A TEMPLAR BOOK

First published in the UK in 2013 by Templar Publishing,
an imprint of the Templar Company Limited,
Deepdene Lodge, Deepdene Avenue, Dorking, Surrey, RH5 4AT, UK
www.templarco.co.uk

ISBN 978-1-84877-873-3

Designed by janie louise hunt
Rewritten by Katie Cotton

Printed in Malaysia

Little
Red Riding
Hood

Alison Jay

templar publishing

Once upon a time

if you wanted a cream cake or an iced bun you
would visit the lovely tea shop in Fairytale Village.
Mrs Hood, the owner, had made her daughter a bright
red cape, which suited the girl so much that everyone in
the village called her Little Red Riding Hood.

One day, Little Red Riding Hood
was on her way to visit her sick grandmother
in her cottage in the woods.
"Don't dawdle," her mother told her as she set off.
"And don't talk to any strangers! Especially not the

Big Bad Wolf.

He loves to eat up little girls just like you."

Little Red Riding
Hood had walked deep into
the heart of the dark forest when
suddenly the Big Bad Wolf appeared!
"Where are you going, little girl?"
he asked, licking his lips.

Little Red Riding Hood was scared.
She thought she had better tell the wolf the truth,
in case he got angry. So she did.
"I am taking these cakes to my poor ill grandmother," she said.

"What a sweet little girl you are!" said the wolf. "I'm sure your grandmother would like some of these beautiful flowers too. Why don't you stay here with me and pick some?"

Little Red Riding Hood agreed that this was a lovely idea. "What a kind wolf," she thought, bending to pick a daisy. "I'm sure everyone in Fairytale Village is wrong about him." But when she looked up, the wolf had gone.

The Big Bad Wolf really was as bad
and greedy as people said, and he had a plan
to gobble Little Red Riding Hood up!
So while Little Red Riding Hood was picking flowers,
he made his way to her grandmother's cottage and locked
up the poor old lady in her wardrobe. Then he put on her
dressing gown, nightcap and glasses, and got into her bed.
"I can't wait for that sweet and juicy Little Red
Riding Hood to arrive," he thought.

A little while later, Little Red Riding Hood came
to the cottage door and saw that it was wide open.
"Is that you, my dear?" called a deep, growly voice from inside.
"Come closer, so I can see you."
So Little Red Riding Hood went closer, and was surprised
to see her grandmother looking quite unlike her normal self.

"Are you feeling a little stronger today, Grandma?"

she asked, inching closer to the bed.

"Why yes, dear," replied the wolf, smiling

dangerously. "In fact, I feel very strong indeed!"

"Oh Grandma," said Little Red Riding Hood.

"What BIG ears you have."

"All the better to hear you with, my dear," said the wolf.

"And Grandma,

what BIG eyes you have."

"All the better to see you with, my dear."

"But Grandma," said Little Red Riding Hood,

"what BIG teeth you have!"

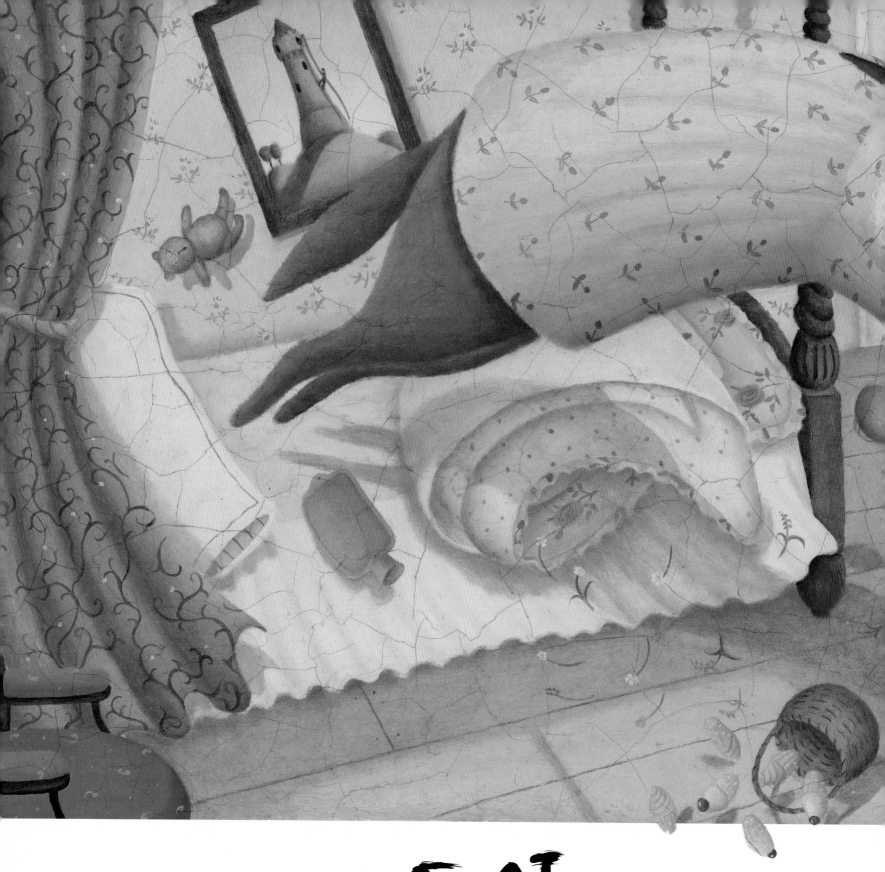

"All the better to **EAT** you with, my dear

red the wolf, leaping out of bed and snapping at Red Riding Hood's little red cape.

Luckily, at that very moment a brave woodcutter
happened to be passing by the cottage. He heard the
wolf's wicked words and came to Red Riding Hood's
rescue in the nick of time. He soon had the
Big Bad Wolf safely tied up outside and
Little Red Riding Hood was overjoyed to discover
her grandmother alive and well in the wardrobe.

Little Red Riding Hood's mother baked the woodcutter his favourite cake as a special thank you for his help.

Everyone in the village was delighted that the Big Bad Wolf had been captured, apart from the wolf himself, of course.

He was taken to a special school
for naughty fairytale creatures, where he was
taught that eating little girls is not very nice,
no matter how sweet and juicy they are.

From then on, Little Red Riding Hood
loved visiting her grandmother even more
because she could play in the
forest as much as she liked!